Wild Water

Personal Watercraft

BY S.L. HAMILTON

McLEAN MERCER REGIONAL LIBRARY
BOX 505
RIVERDALE, ND 58565

A&D Xtreme
An imprint of Abdo Publishing | www.abdopublishing.com

Visit us at
www.abdopublishing.com

Published by Abdo Publishing Company, a division of ABDO, PO Box 398166, Minneapolis, Minnesota 55439. Copyright ©2016 by Abdo Consulting Group, Inc. International copyrights reserved in all countries. No part of this book may be reproduced in any form without written permission from the publisher. A&D Xtreme™ is a trademark and logo of Abdo Publishing Company.

Printed in the United States of America, North Mankato, Minnesota.
052015
092015

 PRINTED ON RECYCLED PAPER

Editor: John Hamilton
Graphic Design: Sue Hamilton
Cover Design: Sue Hamilton
Cover Photo: Kawasaki Motors Corp
Interior Photos: Alamy-pgs 22 & 23; AP-pgs 15 & 30-31; Atlantis Enterprises-pg 30 (lanyard); Bombardier Recreational Products-pg 6 (middle); Dreamstime-pgs 18-19, 19 (top) & 24 (top); Glow Images-pgs 28-29; iStock-pgs 2-3, 12-13, 24 (bottom), 25 (top, middle & bottom) & 32; Kawasaki Motors Corp-pgs 4-5, 6 (bottom), 7 (top), 10-11, 11 (inset), 16-17, 17 (inset) & 19 (middle); Yamaha Watercraft Group-pgs 1, 7 (both middle photos), 8-9, 12 (inset), 14, 19 (bottom), 20-21 & 26-27; Wikimedia/Clayton Jacobson-pg 6 (top).

Websites
To learn more about Wild Water action, visit booklinks.abdopublishing.com. These links are routinely monitored and updated to provide the most current information available.

Library of Congress Control Number: 2015930950

Cataloging-in-Publication Data

Hamilton, S.L.
 Personal watercraft / S.L. Hamilton.
   p. cm. -- (Wild water)
 ISBN 978-1-62403-751-1
 1. Personal watercraft--Juvenile literature.   I. Title.
 797.3--dc23

2015930950

Contents

Personal Watercraft 4
History 6
Safety Equipment 8
Parts of a PWC 10
Engine 12
How to Ride 14
Speed 16
Watercross 18
Freeride/Freestyle 22
Super Course 26
Dangers 28
Glossary 30
Index 32

Personal Watercraft

Today's personal watercraft (PWCs) are like motorcycles for the water. PWCs are used for play, transportation, and racing. Some of the most well-known PWCs are Sea-Doo, Jet Ski, and WaveRunner.

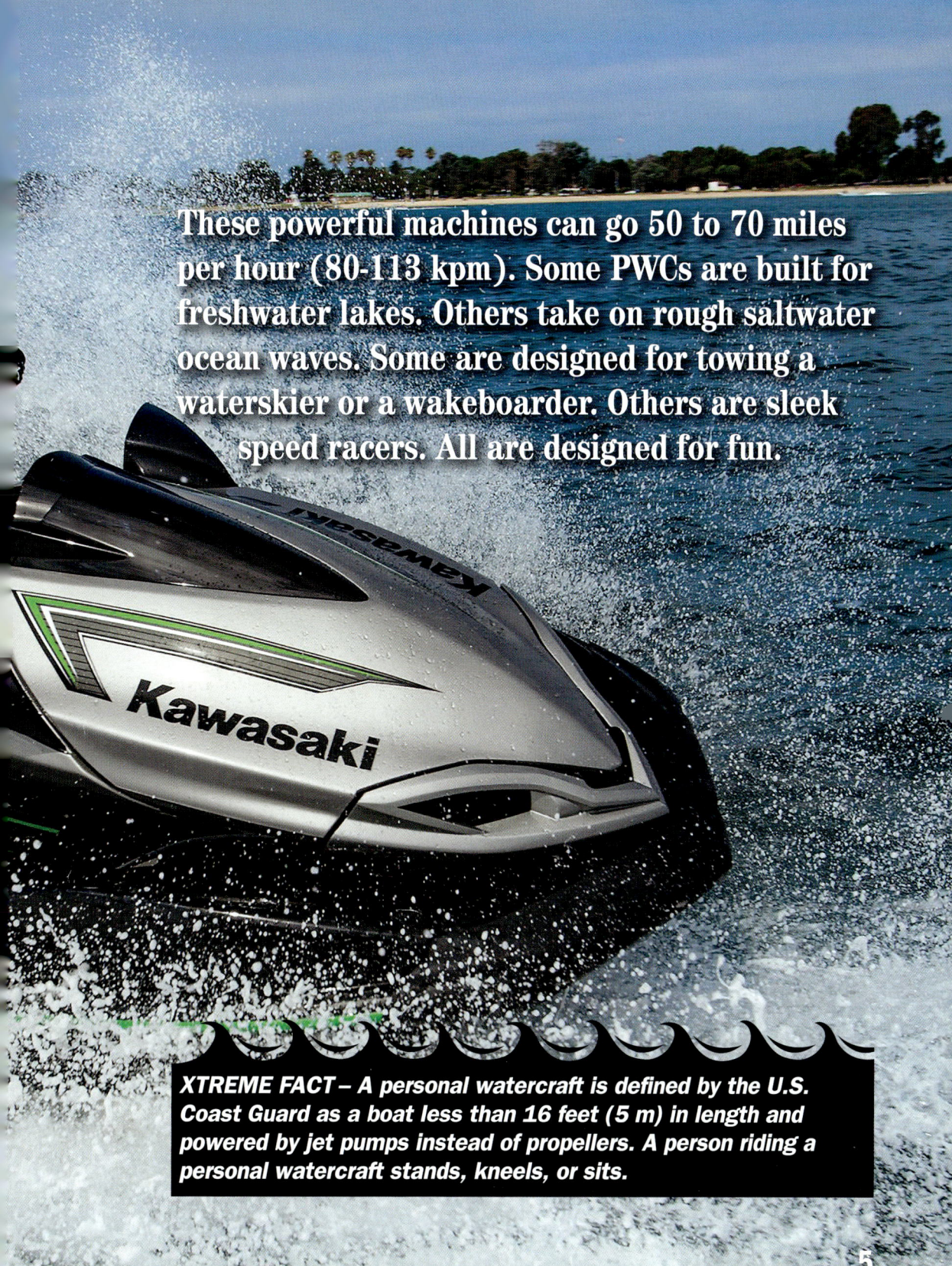

These powerful machines can go 50 to 70 miles per hour (80-113 kpm). Some PWCs are built for freshwater lakes. Others take on rough saltwater ocean waves. Some are designed for towing a waterskier or a wakeboarder. Others are sleek speed racers. All are designed for fun.

XTREME FACT – A personal watercraft is defined by the U.S. Coast Guard as a boat less than 16 feet (5 m) in length and powered by jet pumps instead of propellers. A person riding a personal watercraft stands, kneels, or sits.

History

Clayton Jacobson II designed a powered motorski in the 1960s.

Jacobson's Powered Motorski

BRP Sea-Doo

Jacobson and Bombardier Recreational Products introduced the Sea-Doo in 1968. However, it was difficult to control and had only moderate success.

Kawasaki Jet Ski

In 1971, Jacobson took his ideas to Kawasaki. They introduced the Jet Ski in 1973. The Jet Ski had a powerful 400cc engine and handlebar steering.

Kawasaki Jet Ski

Jet Ski riders felt like they were waterskiing without a boat. However, it was still difficult to stay aboard the tippy PWC.

Yamaha WaveRunner

Yamaha WaveJammer

In 1986 and 1987, Yamaha introduced the WaveRunner and the WaveJammer. They were the first sit-down style PWCs. Bombardier followed with a V-hull Sea-Doo version. Two-person PWCs were also introduced. These styles were more stable and much easier to operate. Suddenly, everyone wanted a fun personal watercraft. The rapidly growing sport peaked in 1995. Today's PWCs range from multi-passenger family models to high-powered sport models.

XTREME FACT – The Sea-Doo became the bestselling boat in the world in the 1990s.

Safety Equipment

Personal watercraft riders must wear life vests approved by the U.S. Coast Guard. These personal flotation devices (PFDs) are designed to keep a person's head above the water, even if they are knocked out. Many riders also wear protective gloves, goggles, and footwear.

XTREME FACT – Some people think water is soft. It actually has a very strong surface tension. At a fast speed, a person who hits water can feel like they are hitting concrete.

Many PWC riders wear helmets. Helmets save lives. Some riders choose a motocross helmet. Others pick a light PWC helmet designed with vents that drain water quickly.

Parts of a PWC

Today's personal watercraft are safer and more adaptable than ever. These machines weigh from 400 to 1,000 pounds (181 to 454 kg). They can go through shallow or deep water. If a PWC tips or rolls over, it will right itself. Manufacturers have decreased noise levels and increased gas mileage.

Bow
The front of the PWC.

Hull
A V-hull allows the PWC to easily cut through the water. This makes it easier to increase speed and reduces the amount of spray in the driver's face. It also allows for sharp turns at higher speeds.

10

Handlebars
The handlebars are connected to the jet propulsion unit, allowing the rider to steer.

Throttle
Controls speed.

Key
The key is on a safety lanyard attached to a driver or safety vest. If the driver is thrown off, the key pulls out, and the PWC stops.

Seat
A PWC seat may be made for 1, 2, or 3 people.

Footwell

Rear Deck
Used to sit to put on waterskies or wakeboards, for climbing aboard, and for gear.

Engine

A PWC uses a gasoline-powered inboard motor to power a screw-shaped impeller that drives water through a water jet pump. This jet action provides a surprising amount of speed and maneuverability.

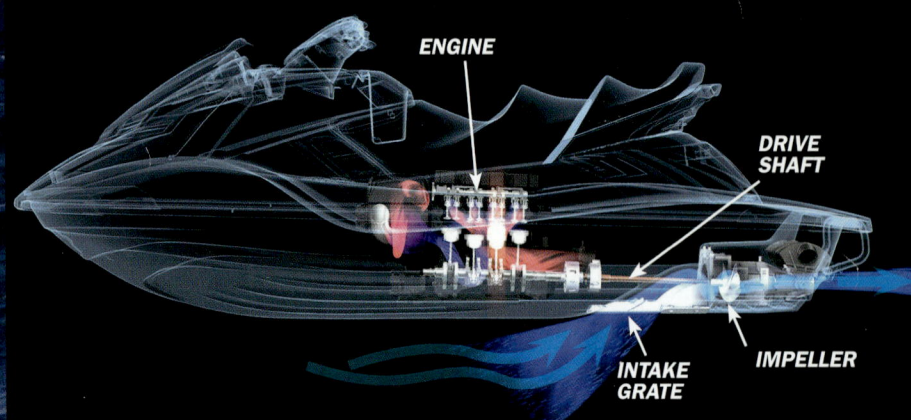

PERSONAL WATERCRAFT PROPULSION

How to Ride

Personal watercraft have cushioned seats, and hulls designed to move easily through the water. Riders choose a comfortable sitting position in slow or calm waters. Multiple riders on one PWC stay sitting for safety.

XTREME QUOTE – "Just because there is a seat doesn't mean you just sit there all the time."
–Erminio Iantosca, World Champions Pro Runabout PWC Division

Many PWCs are ridden fast or in choppy waters. It is much better to stand when riding in these conditions. Standing allows a person's legs to act as shock absorbers against the jolts and jerks of the PWC on the waves. A stand-up position also allows drivers to adjust their feet and body to handle turns.

Speed

Today's personal watercraft are fast enough to tow a waterskier, wakeboarder, or sport tube. Cruising speeds range from 20 to 40 miles per hour (32 to 64 kph). Top speeds are usually about 70 mph (113 kph). Some high-performance vehicles can go as fast as 90 mph (145 kph). It takes an experienced driver to control a PWC going that fast.

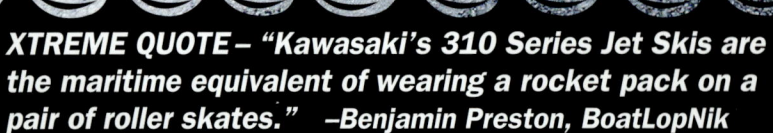

XTREME QUOTE – "Kawasaki's 310 Series Jet Skis are the maritime equivalent of wearing a rocket pack on a pair of roller skates." –Benjamin Preston, BoatLopNik

Some PWCs are designed with color-coded keys so the driver can only go up to a certain speed. A yellow SLO mode key reduces the engine power by 30 percent. A green key is full-power mode. This can be dangerously fast for inexperienced drivers. It's important that drivers realize that if they are traveling at 90 mph (145 kph), they will cover a mile (1.6 km) in just 40 seconds.

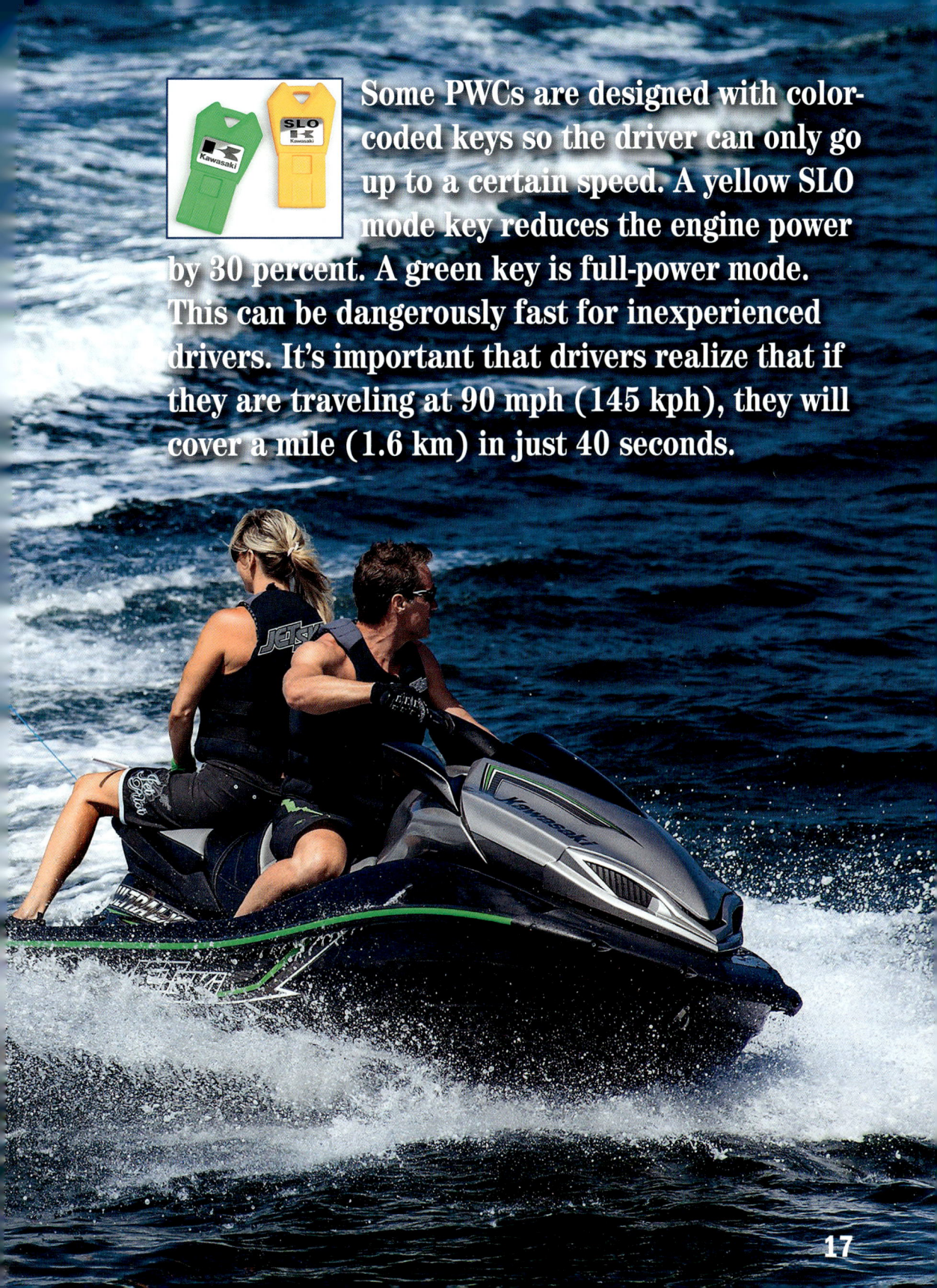

Watercross

Watercross is like a motorcycle race on the water. A closed-course event pits racers against each other beginning from a side-by-side start. Speeds may reach 90 miles per hour (145 kph) on ½- to ¾-mile (.8- to 1.2-km) tracks. It is fast and dangerous. Watercross may be held on rivers, lakes, oceans, and some indoor arenas.

XTREME FACT – The International Jet Sports Boating Association (IJSBA) is the governing body of personal watercraft racing.

Watercross Divisions

Ski Division

The Ski Division uses PWCs made for one standing person. The vehicle is steered from a moveable hand pole that rises up and holds the handlebars.

Sport Division

The Sport Division uses PWCs that are made for one person with a seat and a fixed handlebar.

Runabout Division

Runabouts are powerful PWCs for one or more people. They have a fixed handlebar, and a hull width greater than 38 inches (97 cm).

A watercross closed-course layout may be small with sharp turns, or large with fewer turns and more straightaways. The beginning of the race may have competitors split into separate lanes for safety. Inflatable white buoys called "hot dogs" show racers where to merge from their separate lanes.

A yellow buoy indicates a right turn. Two or more yellow buoys indicate a larger sweeping right turn.

A checkered buoy indicates the start and finish line. Racers must go between these checkered buoys on every lap.

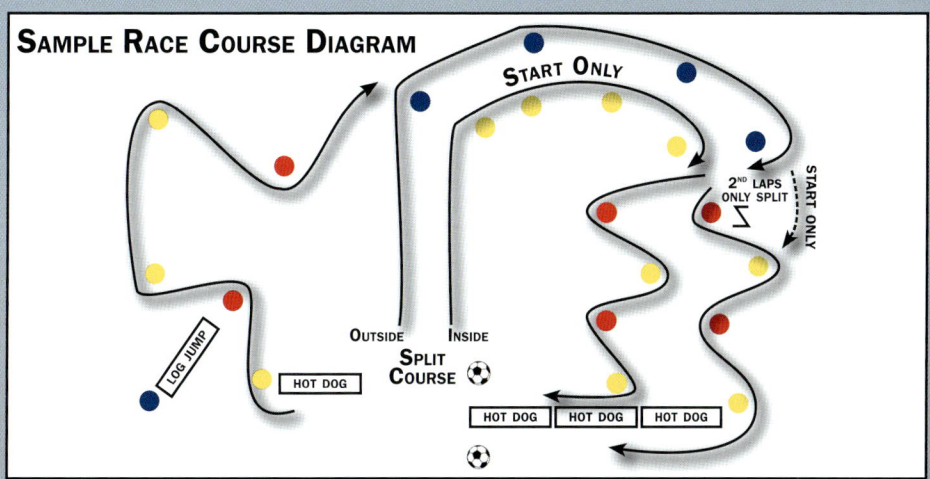

SAMPLE RACE COURSE DIAGRAM

Some courses and race tracks have obstacles. Expert and pro ski racers jump over these obstacles. A "log jump," for example, is usually a tire anchored in the water.

A red buoy indicates a left turn. Two or more red buoys indicate a larger, sweeping left turn.

Freeride/Freestyle

Freeride or freestyle is a form of stand-up watercraft competition in which the rider performs tricks and stunts with the vehicle. Certain competition PWCs are built just for freeriding. The Yamaha SuperJet is used by many competitors.

Freerider routines commonly last for two minutes. They are judged and scored by experts watching on land. These competitions, such as Australia's Rip 'n Ride, are usually open to all ages and both male and female competitors.

Freeriders perform various tricks in their stunt routines. They do spins, flips, dives, and barrel rolls. Each has its own degree of difficulty. Some stunts are even performed backwards or partially underwater.

XTREME FACT – *There are many fun names for freerider tricks: power submarine, Hollywood corkscrew, kilowatt flop, ride 'em cowboy, bull doggin', aerial barrel roll, backflips, nosedives, 360s, and spins. Some sound like they come from a rodeo, and others from an amusement park ride, but all are challenging stunts that require great skill.*

Super Course

Super course, or offshore racing, is a long-distance personal watercraft race. It is a challenge of a driver's toughness and a PWCs endurance. Riders may compete in a point-to-point race or a multiple-lap race around a specific course. Races may be as long as 300 miles (483 km). Some races allow for pit stops for refueling, while others do not.

Super course races are popular since they do not involve much contact between drivers. However, the length of time on the water can be very tiring. Not only must racers stay focused for hours, they must also be aware of water conditions. This determines how fast to go in order to conserve fuel. Those who miscalculate often run out of gas and must be towed in.

XTREME FACT – The Mark Hahn Memorial 300 is known as the world's longest PWC race. It is named after endurance racer Mark Hahn, who died while PWC racing in 2004. It is sponsored by the IJSBA and is held in Lake Havasu, Arizona. Each lap is 10 miles (16 k). There are several team events, but the individual "Ironman" race is the most intense. To date, racer Craig Warner holds the fastest time at 4 hours, 31 minutes, 24 seconds.

Dangers

Most PWC accidents occur when riders are unexpectedly flung off their vehicles. In addition, a PWC might hit submerged objects, make unexpected turns, encounter rough waves, or simply be driven too fast.

Serious and even deadly accidents take place when a PWC is going 40 mph (64 kph) or more. But even at slower speeds, an uncontrolled water entry can cause a person to be knocked unconscious. It can also result in a concussion, broken bones, ruptured organs, or even death. Safety training is a vital part of being a PWC driver or rider.

XTREME FACT – The best way to hit the water is with legs and feet together, toes down, arms crossed and pulled in tightly to the chest, and as vertical as possible.

Glossary

Freshwater
Water sources with little amounts of salt in them, such as lakes and rivers. Saltwater, such as water in oceans and seas, has a higher salt content.

IJSBA
The International Jet Sports Boating Association is the governing agency for personal watercraft racing. The IJSBA promotes, organizes, and supervises PWC events around the world, including freestyle and endurance races.

Lanyard
A key holder that attaches to a PWC driver and the vehicle. If a driver is thrown off the vehicle, the lanyard pulls out the key and stops the vehicle. A lanyard may also hold a whistle, which a dislodged rider uses to help locate him or her in the water.

Motocross
A type of motorcycle race that uses dirt bikes on a rugged cross-country track. Motocross helmets are sometimes worn by personal watercraft riders.

Personal Flotation Device (PFD)
Also known as a life jacket. A life-saving device designed to keep a person afloat even if he or she has been knocked out. Different styles are available to allow needed freedom of movement for boaters, canoers, kayakers, and PWC riders.

Propulsion
How something moves. A PWC uses an inboard engine to power a water jet pump, which makes the vehicle move.

Saltwater
Water with a heavier salt content than freshwater, about 35 parts per thousand. It is found in Earth's seas and oceans.

Shock Absorbers
Usually a device that takes the bumps and jolts created by a motorized vehicle. On a PWC, a standing rider's legs act as shock absorbers against the bumps created by going through waves and water.

Spin
A trick where the driver makes the PWC circle around a half turn (180 degrees), or a full turn (360 degrees).

Unconscious
A person who is not awake or aware of what is going on around them.

Index

A
Arizona 27
Australia 23

B
BoatLopNik 16
Bombardier Recreational Products 6, 7

C
Coast Guard, U.S. 5, 8

F
freeride 22, 23, 24, 25
freestyle 22

H
Hahn, Mark 27

I
Iantosca, Erminio 14
IJSBA (International Jet Sports Boating Association) 18, 27
Ironman (race) 27

J
Jacobson, Clayton II 6
Jet Ski 4, 6, 7, 16

K
Kawasaki 6, 7, 16

L
Lake Havasu, AZ 27
lanyard 11

M
Mark Hahn Memorial 300 (race) 27
motocross 9

O
offshore racing 26

P
Preston, Benjamin 16

R
Rip 'n Ride 23
Runabout Division (watercross) 19

S
Sea-Doo 4, 6, 7
shock absorbers 15
Ski Division, (watercross) 19
Sport Division, (watercross) 19
super course 26, 27
SuperJet (Yamaha) 22

T
310 Series (Kawasaki Jet Skis) 16

W
Warner, Craig 27
watercross 18, 19, 20
WaveJammer 7
WaveRunner 4, 7
World Champions Pro Runabout PWC Division 14

Y
Yamaha 7, 22

32